CORAL REEFS

EARTH'S UNDERSEA TREASURES

LAURENCE PRINGLE

SIMON & SCHUSTER BOOKS FOR YOUNG READERS

Picture Credits

Map p. 14 by Robert Romagnoli.
Photographs: Christy Gavitt, p. 8, 9, 18, 21, 22, 25, 27 *(left and bottom right)*, 28, 35, 40; Cristina Kessler, p. 2. Photographs from Visuals Unlimited: Hal Beral, p. 10, 13 *(top)*, 34; D. Cavagnaro, p. 16; R. DeGoursey, p. 32; Dave B. Fleetham, pp. 4–5, 6, 13 *(bottom)*, 24, 27 *(top right)*, 31, 39; John Forsythe, endpapers; Kjell Sandved, p. 36; Marty Snyderman, p. 30.

Frontispiece: *Coral reef partners: a clownfish and a sea anemone*

SIMON & SCHUSTER BOOKS FOR YOUNG READERS
An imprint of Simon & Schuster Children's Publishing Division
1230 Avenue of the Americas
New York, New York 10020
SIMON & SCHUSTER BOOKS FOR YOUNG READERS
is a trademark of Simon & Schuster.

Book design by Anahid Hamparian
The text for this book is set in 13 point Aldine 401.

Manufactured in Hong Kong
10 9 8 7 6 5 4 3 2 1

Library of Congress Cataloging-in-Publication Data
Pringle, Laurence P.
  Coral reefs / Laurence Pringle
    p. cm.
Summary: Explores coral reef systems and their relationship to fish and other ocean life.
  ISBN 0-689-80286-2
  1. Coral reef ecology—Juvenile literature. [1. Coral reef ecology. 2. Ecology.] I. Title.
QH541.5.C7P75 1995 574.5'26367—dc20 94-5875

CONTENTS

Oragon moray eels at home in a Hawaiian reef (left).

RAIN FORESTS OF THE SEA

ACCORDING TO HAWAIIAN LEGEND, the god Kumuhonua created all of the fish and gave each kind a role or duty to perform. Then, in order to tell them apart, he called all the fish together and gave them colors and names. One was especially beautiful, with light blue fins and gold, black, blue, and red bars and stripes on its body. Kumuhonua gave it the longest name of any fish on earth: *humuhumu-nukunuku-a-pua's,* which means "the fish that carries a needle and has a snout and grunts like a pig."

The *humuhumu-nukunuku-a-pua's* was once Hawaii's state fish. It is actually a triggerfish, and it does carry a needle—a stout spine on its back. When danger threatens, a triggerfish dashes into a tight-fitting crevice, erects the spine, and locks it in place with another, smaller "trigger" spine. No amount of pulling or tugging will budge the triggerfish.

The god Kumuhonua had quite a task, giving names, colors, and roles to Hawaii's fish. Nearly four hundred species live on the coral reefs of Hawaii.

Kumuhonua could be thankful, however, that he was not god in Palau, a string of islands in the western Pacific. The coral reefs there are home to fifteen hundred species of fish and seven hundred species of coral.

A bewildering variety of animals lives in, on, or near coral reefs. In fact, the rich variety of life on coral reefs prompts biologists to call reefs "the rain forests of the sea." Tropical rain forests harbor earth's greatest diversity of animal species, especially of insects, spiders, and other *invertebrates.* Coral reefs, on the other hand, are home to a greater variety of animal groups: fish, crabs, sponges, starfish, sea urchins, *mollusks,* shrimps, anemones, and corals themselves. Most of these groups do not occur on land.

The complex animal-plant communities of both reefs and rain forests hold many mysteries. Both are homes of species still unknown to humans. Both hold clues to understanding nature, and perhaps to developing new medicines for people.

"The fish that carries a needle and has a snout and grunts like a pig."

Both, too, are being destroyed or threatened by humans.

Close to shore in shallow waters, coral reefs are especially vulnerable to pollution and overfishing. They can even be damaged by people who dive down to observe the life that reefs attract and sustain, which occurs in colors and forms beyond imagination. The unique life of coral reefs may also be threatened by human-made changes in the earth's atmosphere.

Perhaps the most beautiful and fascinating *habitats* anywhere on earth, coral reefs are one of our planet's greatest treasures. People must find ways to safeguard them.

A school of bighead jacks passes over clownfish swimming close to a Red Sea reef.

In the evening, tentacles begin to emerge from the mouths of star corals.

A VITAL PARTNERSHIP

CORAL REEFS ARE THE OLDEST, MOST diverse, and most productive habitats in the sea. They exist because certain kinds of tiny coral animals are able to take dissolved salts from seawater and convert them into calcium carbonate, usually called limestone. These coral animals are called hard corals or stony corals.

A coral animal is called a *polyp*. Most *species* are less than 1 inch wide, though polyps of the mushroom coral measure 6 inches across. Related to jellyfish and sea anemones, corals are a lot like miniature anemones. Their soft bodies resemble a double-walled balloon. The polyps of hard corals are encased in a limestone skeleton that is open at the top.

Coral animals are stuck in one place, like plants. In fact, for many centuries corals were believed to *be* plants. Not until the eighteenth century were they correctly classified as animals. Coral polyps are "sit-and-wait" *predators*. Their mouths are ringed by tentacles. On the tentacles are hundreds of stinging cells.

Tiny *crustaceans* that drift within reach are stung, captured, and swallowed by the coral polyps.

The little crustaceans and other small creatures that corals eat are called *zooplankton*. Most of these microscopic animals hide in or near reefs during the daytime, then at night rise into the open water to feed on tiny drifting plants. Since zooplankton are most plentiful in reef waters at night, most reef-building corals withdraw their tentacles during the day. Coral colonies look like odd plants or even rocks by day, when most people swim close to reefs. At night their surfaces come alive with the waving tentacles of millions of coral animals.

True reef-building coral polyps do not catch all of the food they need in order to thrive and grow. The rest comes from within their own soft, transparent tissues, where microscopic *algae* live. It is the algae, called *zooxanthellae* (pronounced zoh-ZAN-thel-ly), that give coral polyps their brilliant colors—and much more.

This partnership benefits both the animals and the

Coral animals have hundreds of tiny stinging cells on their tentacles.

algae. From polyps the algae get shelter and wastes that nourish them. The wastes include phosphorus and carbon dioxide, a gas given off as polyps digest their food. Using energy from the sun, the algae convert carbon dioxide and water into oxygen and carbohydrates, both of which benefit the polyps.

The partnership between coral polyps and zooxanthellae is complex. Marine scientists are still trying to understand it. They agree, however, that this partnership between simple animals and microscopic algae makes reef building possible. Without their algae, coral polyps make little or no limestone. Even though polyps are animals, they depend on sunlight for their growth as much as green plants do.

Zooxanthellae are most concentrated in the tentacles of polyps, where they get maximum exposure to sunlight. Algae need solar energy in order to make food, so reef-building corals live no deeper than 250 feet. When a diver descends 100 feet or so, he or she notices hard corals becoming less varied and abundant.

There are other kinds of corals that live in dim light or even in constant darkness. They feed on zooplankton and have no algae within their cells. Some are hard corals that secrete small amounts of limestone and usually live in dark places of reefs. Divers find them on the ceilings of reef caves and on overhangs.

Others are soft corals. They include sea fans, sea feathers, sea plumes, and sea whips. They can live at depths far beyond the reach of sunlight. Soft corals have been found nearly 4 miles beneath the ocean surface. They often feed during the daytime, and grow bountifully where strong currents carry plentiful *plankton.*

Soft corals are able to expel water and shrink into dense blobs, and then later absorb water and expand into large, colorful forms with countless waving tentacles. In *Reef: A Safari Through the Coral World,* author Jeremy Stafford-Deitsch wrote of his first encounter, in the Red Sea, with this ability of soft corals. His diving companion pointed out some darkly colored blobs that Jeremy looked at briefly. They swam on to explore an area of stony corals. Then a strong current began to flow, and Jeremy "realized we would have to swim around that drab point again to get back to the boat."

He swam in what he thought was the right direction, but the reef looked dramatically different: "Great billowing, meter-high, multi-colored corals were everywhere. Some were yellow, others orange, some rich purple."

Jeremy was surprised when the current carried him to the dive boat. His partner cleared up his confusion, explaining that "the boring blobs we saw at the start of the dive were in fact retracted soft corals; as soon as there is a current, they swell with seawater, expand and feed."

Reef-building corals thrive in sunlit, warm salty water. They can live in seawater temperatures of 61–97° F (16–36° C) but grow best in the narrow range of 73–77° F (23–25° C). Coral reefs are found mostly in the tropics and in areas where warm currents flow out of the tropics. The north-flowing Gulf Stream, for instance, brings warm water to the shores of Florida and Bermuda, enabling corals to grow there.

A world map that shows where reefs occur (see page 14) reveals an odd pattern: almost no reefs on the western coasts of continents. This is the result of cold ocean currents. Off California and Mexico, for example, the south-flowing California Current is too chilly for corals. About 60 percent of all coral reefs are found in the Indian Ocean, including the Red Sea. A quarter of all reefs on earth grow in the Pacific Ocean, and the rest occur mostly in the Caribbean.

As sea currents flow around them, colonies of soft coral swell to their full size and beauty.

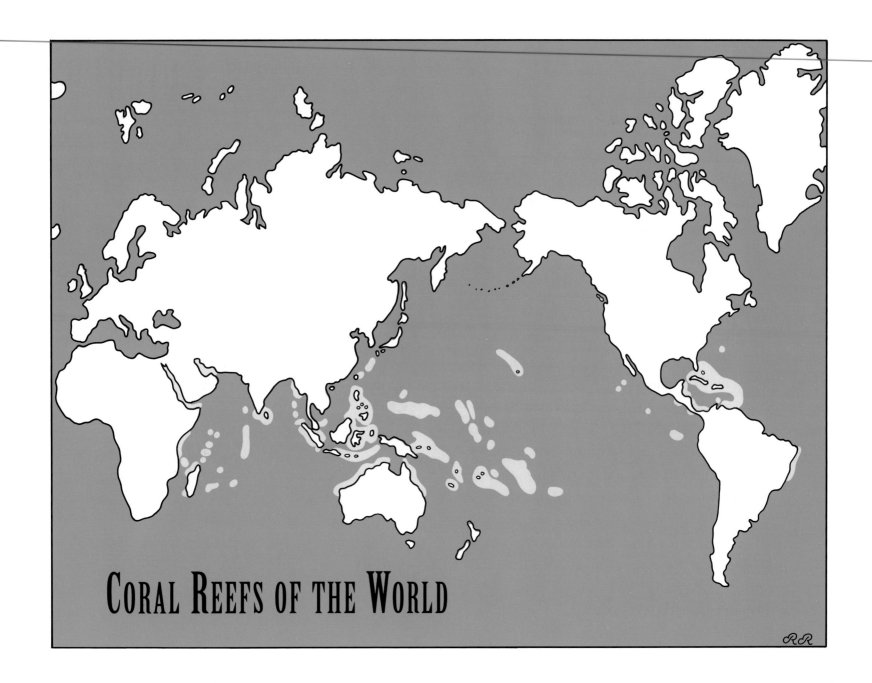

CORAL REEFS OF THE WORLD

MASTER BUILDERS

FINGERS AND HORNS, EVEN BRAINS and lettuce leaves—the names of hard corals describe their distinctive shapes. Their forms can vary, however, depending on the environment in which they live. The elkhorn coral of the Caribbean, for example, does not always look like elk antlers. Where waves are strong, it and other hard corals tend to be short and squat, with rounded or flattened shapes. It only grows in its most slender, fragile form in places where it is usually sheltered from the waves.

Even in such places, corals with gracefully branching shapes can be damaged by storms. Hurricanes Allen (1980), Gilbert (1988), and Hugo (1989) smashed many staghorn corals that grew in Discovery Bay on the north coast of Jamaica in the Caribbean. We usually picture hurricanes battering the land, but they can cause damage underwater, too, as waves topple corals 140 feet beneath the surface. Hurricanes also stir up sand and silt that bury some corals and harm others. Though staghorns grow more quickly than

Coral reefs grow in areas, shown in gold, where seawater is warm year-round.

most corals, they may need a half century in order to dominate Discovery Bay as they once did.

A person swimming over a healthy reef may look down on a bewildering display of more than a dozen kinds of hard corals. This riot of colors and shapes looks like an underwater garden. What appears to be paradise, however, is really a battleground where different kinds of corals compete for space and light.

Where two coral colonies grow side by side, there is usually a band of white, dead coral—where polyps have died—that belongs to one or the other colony. A colony under attack on one flank may be attacking in another direction. Some species release digestive juices that kill a competitor's polyps. One Pacific Ocean species responds to attack by growing extralong "sweeper" tentacles with powerful stings that destroy any part of a competing colony they touch. All over a reef, coral colonies are engaged in silent, slow-motion warfare.

No two coral reefs are alike, but there are three basic types. They were first described by Charles

Darwin after the historic global journey (1831–1836) of HMS *Beagle,* on which he served as the scientific observer. Most of Darwin's ideas about coral reefs have stood the test of time.

Fringing reefs grow along coasts or around islands that have a sharp drop-off to deep water near their shores. Most of the corals grow near the edge of the drop-off. A lagoon of shallow water, called a reef flat, lies between the fringing reef and the land. Reef flats are often littered with rubble of broken coral.

Some of the most extraordinary fringing reefs occur in the Red Sea, where a seawall plunges sharply just a short distance offshore of the hot Egyptian desert. There is little rain to wash silt onto coral animals and few clouds to block solar energy. As a result, a rich variety of corals flourishes in fringing reefs close to shore.

Barrier reefs also develop along the edges of islands or continents, but usually are farther from land than fringing reefs. They are separated from the land by a wide, deep lagoon. These reefs usually stretch for many miles and form unbroken barriers that slow the ocean's powerful waves. The world's best-known example, the Great Barrier Reef, is actually not a true barrier reef. It is a complex series of nearly three thousand reefs that stretch along more than 1,200 miles of Australia's northeast coast. The outermost reefs lie

Kure Atoll, west of Hawaii.

between 20 and 150 miles offshore. Coral reefs do protect Australia's coast, but they do not form a continuous barrier.

In 1835 Charles Darwin wrote of the third main kind of coral reef: "We saw several of those most curious rings of coral land, just rising above the water's edge, which have been called Lagoon Islands." Today they are called atolls, and they are found mostly in the Pacific Ocean.

Atolls begin when a volcano erupts from the ocean floor. After it reaches the surface, a fringing reef grows around it. Over many thousands of years, the seafloor sinks from the weight of the dormant volcano, which is also eroded away by rain and waves. Rising sea levels may also cause more of the volcanic island to disappear beneath the surface. As the island shrinks, its surrounding lagoon grows larger. The fringing reef gradually becomes a barrier reef. Eventually the last of the island vanishes beneath the waves. A ring of reef remains with a lagoon but little or no land in its center.

Coral animals settle down and grow wherever they can, and not always at the site of a fringing or barrier reef, or an atoll. For instance, in deep lagoons or on continental shelves, there may be rock outcroppings that are close enough to the surface for corals to grow on them. Reefs in such scattered locations are called patch reefs.

Many odd-shaped patch reefs rise from the bottom of Micronesia's Truk Lagoon. In 1944, during World War II, U.S. Navy aircraft launched a surprise attack on part of Japan's Imperial Fourth Fleet. Bombs and torpedoes sank four destroyers and dozens of supply ships and other vessels. The lagoon floor became a metal marine graveyard. The surfaces of hulls, masts, cables, deck guns, and anchor chains are now covered with multicolored life: hard and soft corals, anemones, and sponges.

A coral reef is another kind of marine graveyard. Its upper surface teems with life, but the great bulk of it is made up of stony remains of hard corals, and of other organisms, too. Sponges, mollusks, sea urchins, starfish, and other marine animals have the ability to take chemicals from seawater and make stony materials.

They don't deposit layer after layer as hard corals do, but the remains of their own limestone or other stony materials often become part of a reef. Clams and other mollusks leave their shells. Others leave microscopic stony rods that had supported their soft bodies.

Even plants, including certain kinds of algae and seaweed, leave behind calcium carbonate when they die. Coralline algae is very important to a coral reef. It needs less sunlight than zooxanthellae and can grow in dimly lit areas of a reef. This plant acts like a layer of cement over parts of a reef and helps protect it from erosion.

All of these organisms contribute to a coral reef's existence, but it is the reef-building corals that play the most vital role. Most of them grow slowly. The star coral of the Caribbean takes a century to grow 3 feet. Boulder coral expands at about the same pace. And yet, given enough time, coral animals are the master builders of the earth.

Millions of years ago, coral animals built what geologists named Key Largo limestone, the foundation rock of the curving string of islands called the Florida Keys. Parts of the Great Barrier Reef are twenty million years old, but its most recent growth began just nine thousand years ago when sea levels rose. Plains then off Australia's coast were flooded, allowing coral colonies to build on the ancient foundations of this huge reef system.

The Great Barrier Reef is visible from the moon and even farther away in space. No human-made structure is.

A WEALTH OF LIFE IN A POOR NEIGHBORHOOD

THE EARLIEST FORMS OF HARD CORALS lived in warm shallow seas about 450 million years ago. The remains of reefs they built in shallow seas are sometimes found far inland. Geologists have discovered evidence of coral reefs in Illinois, Indiana, and Wisconsin. About 250 million years ago, a large barrier reef thrived where west Texas is now.

Many kinds of corals died out sixty-five million years ago, during the same period in which the dinosaurs died out. This great global extinction may have been caused by a 10-mile-wide asteroid smashing into earth. Dust and debris from this huge explosion changed climates and disrupted food chains, including those upon which coral animals relied. New coral species evolved from the survivors. In the foothills of the Italian Alps, scientists have found the remains of corals and many fossil fish that lived about fifty million years ago. The corals and fish fossils are remarkably like those that live today.

Worldwide, about seven hundred kinds of reef-build-ing corals exist today. However, a person diving to reefs off Florida or in the Caribbean sees only a few dozen kinds of hard corals. These reef communities are comparatively young. Reefs with much longer histories have many more kinds of corals, and other creatures as well. A single reef in the western Pacific or Indian Ocean may harbor two hundred kinds of corals and more than fifty species of butterfly fish. In contrast, just five kinds of butterfly fish live in the Caribbean.

The astonishing variety of life found in, on, and near coral reefs once puzzled scientists. They wondered how such a wealth of living things could exist in warm shallow seas, which usually contain very little nitrogen, phosphorus, or other *nutrients* that living things need. Tropical ocean waters have been called "nutrient deserts." Yet they support reefs that are among the most productive *ecosystems* on earth.

The answer to this apparent paradox lies in the complex food webs of the reef communities. Every

The oldest reef communities may be home to more than fifty kinds of butterfly fish.

bit of nitrogen and other nutrients is recycled by the plants and animals of reefs. Nothing, not even fish droppings, goes to waste.

Also, scientist have learned that reefs are not the isolated ecosystems they once were thought to be. Many are fairly close to land. As a result, the waters around them receive more nutrients than the open ocean. Furthermore, there are reef bases, lagoons, sea-grass prairies, and other nearby habitats that play big roles in coral reef food webs.

Coral is a soft rock that easily erodes into sand or is ground into sand when ingested by fish. Therefore, living reefs often border large areas of coral rubble and sand, both of which also support life. While studying a sand slope beneath a Red Sea reef, marine biologist Eugenie Clark discovered a colony of ten thousand garden eels.

In an article for *Sea Frontiers* magazine, she wrote that during the day, "the silvery-gray eels can stretch almost full length out of their burrows like stalks of willowy sea plants. Their graceful bodies arched, eyes alert for planktonic food, they curtsy and dip, bow and sway performing a tireless dance to the orchestration of invisible currents."

Eugenie Clark and other biologists have identified several new species of fish from this sandy habitat, which would not exist if coral reefs were not eroding above it.

In the Red Sea and wherever reefs occur, some fish hunt for food in other habitats, and then bring nutrients back to their reefs. For example, near Saint Croix in the Caribbean, schools of French and white grunts leave reefs at sunset and catch zooplankton over surrounding beds of sea grass. With full guts they return in the morning and rest over favorite places on their reefs. As they digest food, they excrete nitrogen and other nutrients right over the corals. Biologists discovered that corals with resident fish schools grow faster than those without fish schools.

A coral reef may be many feet thick, but only its outer surface is a thin veneer of living polyps. As each polyp deposits a new floor of limestone over the old one, the entire colony grows upward and outward. A living reef is constantly under construction. It must be, in order to recover from damage caused by storms and by nibbling and rasping mouths.

Some kinds of sponges bore into corals by secreting chemicals that break down limestone. Other animals chew or drill holes in a reef's stony foundation. Clams and other mollusks bore holes in the rock. Marine worms drill holes and often live in great abundance, unseen, within reefs. One 6-pound chunk of dead coral from the Great Barrier Reef contained 1,441 worms from 103 different species!

An estimated 40 percent of coral reefs is not substance but space. Coral reefs are apartment houses, riddled with big and little living spaces. Some may hold large fish or an octopus; others protect microscopic zooplankton. All together, a reef's crevices, nooks, and crannies provide homes for an amazing wealth of life.

A green sea turtle finds shelter in a coral reef.

FISH OF THE REEF

AT AUSTRALIA'S ONE TREE REEF, biologists identified nearly 150 species of fish in an area of about 180 square feet. Worldwide, there are more than four thousand kinds of reef fish, and each year new species are discovered. (A biologist must catch and kill an unusual-looking fish in order to examine it closely, take measurements, and compare it with known species before the fish can be declared to be a new species.)

Reef fish range in size from 1/2-inch-long gobies to 9-foot-long sharks. Anyone who dives down to explore coral reefs is delighted with the color and movement of the fish. Most are active during the day and many allow people to swim close.

Some fish of the open sea, such as jacks and certain kinds of sharks, visit reefs for something to eat. Others use reefs for shelter but feed in other habitats. Nevertheless, most of the fish seen hovering or darting or grazing spend most of their lives in the reef environment. The only time they are away is when they are young. Then they go through a pelagic, or open-water, *larval* stage that is remarkably different from the rest of their lives.

This stage may last a few days or more than a hundred, and a larval fish may travel a few yards or hundreds of miles from the reef where it hatched from an egg. The experience differs greatly from one species to another. One thing is certain: Very few of the little fish survive to become adults.

As newly hatched larval fish leave a reef, they pass through a "wall of mouths." In open water they are chased by many creatures, including tuna and other fish. Days or months later they run another gauntlet of predators as they settle on a reef. However, female reef fish produce huge numbers of eggs, sometimes over a million a year, guaranteeing that some larval fish will survive and become adult reef dwellers.

In the open sea, larvae of some species of fish are pale, almost transparent, and are armed with long fin spines. After settling on a reef, they undergo quick and

Crevalle jacks swim near the reefs of Cocos Island, west of Costa Rica.

dramatic changes, growing scales and developing color in a few days. Some little fish hide in holes or bury themselves in sand while these changes occur. Other species, such as grunts and drums, remain colorless for some time. Still others, such as the great barracuda, develop into good-sized juvenile fish even before settling into their reef habitat.

People have wondered how reef fish, so varied and abundant, can coexist in their compact habitats. One answer lies in reef habitats and their surroundings, which provide a wide range of conditions and so much shelter in a small area. Another answer lies in the adaptations, including behavior, of the fish.

Fish vary not only in their foods but also in the ways in which they get them. Some predators actively hunt, while others wait to ambush their prey. Some feed during the day and sleep at night; others do the reverse. (Some have a time-sharing arrangement for a hideout: night-sleeping fish and day-sleeping fish share the same spot.)

Dawn and dusk are dramatic times, full of change—and danger. Fish are on the move, either

A whitetip reef shark hunts close to the surface of a Hawaiian reef.

going out to feed, or returning to shelter. Some just swim from one part of a reef to another, while others arrive from nearby feeding grounds. At dusk the smallest fish usually hide before sunset. Larger kinds move closer to shelter as the light dims and mill around before settling down for the night. For a few minutes the reef seems deserted. Then the nocturnal fish emerge and spread out over the reef, and beyond.

Reef fish are most vulnerable during these changeover times, so this is when sharks, jacks, and other large predators strike. Jacks sometimes hunt in packs, moving swiftly just above the reef surface, pouncing on any slow or careless prey. Whitetip reef sharks hunt in a reef's caves and crevices, while gray reef sharks seek vulnerable prey above the reef. Gray reef sharks sometimes herd a school of fish up against a reef wall, and then attack.

To avoid being eaten, some plankton-eating fish stay close to the reef surface and dash to cover when jacks or other predators appear. Other plankton feeders roam farther from the reef, but, biologists have observed, these fish have more streamlined bodies and deeply forked tail fins than the species that feed close to the reef. Those that feed close to the reef do not need to be built for speed; fish that range farther out do.

Surprisingly, damselfish are plankton feeders that lack streamlined shapes and do not stay close to their reef hideouts. They seem to be protected from predators in another way, by having very deep (tall and flat-sided) bodies with long, stiff fin spines. This makes them difficult, and painful, to swallow.

Although such reef fish as puffers and wrasses eat both plant and animal food, most adult fish can be put into one of five feeding categories.

Algae is the food of blennies, surgeonfish, parrot fish, and some damselfish. Parrot fish are named for their gaudy colors and beaklike jaws. They were once thought to be carnivores, since they chew on coral. Instead they scrape and nibble algae from coral surfaces. In the process, however, they sometimes do

Soldier fish sleep by day in the shelter of a reef, then emerge at dusk to feed on plankton.

swallow both dead coral and live polyps. Limestone that parrot fish eat is later expelled from their bodies as fine sand.

Surgeonfish (also known as tangs) stand guard over patches of algae on which they feed, but the undisputed champion defenders of algal turf are damselfish. They chase away any plant eater from their algae garden. Apparently, people in diving gear look like plant eaters to damselfish, because these fish, no more than 4 inches long, bang into face masks, nip at skin, and pull hair in order to drive the huge intruders off.

Zooplankton is the food of jewelfish, fusiliers, cardinalfish, and some damselfish. In cloudlike schools, cardinalfish feed on tiny drifting zooplankton near reefs at night. Schools of fusiliers hunt the same prey in daytime.

Corals, sponges, and *anemones* are the food of angelfish and butterfly fish, which are among the most beautiful of all reef fish. Butterfly fish are usually seen in pairs, and are believed to mate for life. Their long snouts enable them to probe into the limestone skeletons of living corals and eat the polyps.

Mollusks, crustaceans, starfish, and *sea urchins* are the food of snappers, pufferfish, triggerfish, box fish, and stingrays, as well as some wrasses. Triggerfish push over coral rubble on the sea bottom and also blow sand away to uncover hiding prey. Triggerfish and pufferfish specialize in eating sea urchins. They and the humpheaded wrasse also kill and eat the crown-of-thorns starfish, which eats live coral animals and has wiped out corals in some parts of the Great Barrier Reef.

Finally, fish themselves are the food of groupers, barracudas, hawkfish, moray eels, and others. Reef fish are also prey of other animals, including sea snakes, seabirds, cone snails, mantis shrimps, some anemones, and some starfish. The brittle star waits in ambush with the center of its body raised, offering a sheltered place for small fish. When a fish enters, the starfish's arms clench tight, and the shelter becomes a prison, where the fish is digested.

Mantis shrimps are about 5 inches long. They are nighttime reef predators. Some species have hammerlike appendages that smash the bodies of crabs and snails. Others have sharply pointed appendages that can pierce a 1-inch piece of wood. Mantis shrimps are remarkable because of the speed with which they strike their prey. They lash out in less than 4 milliseconds (4/1000 of a second)—one of the fastest movements known in the animal kingdom.

Somehow it seems appropriate that such an extraordinary animal as the mantis shrimp lives on coral reefs, where just about any behavior, relationship, or physical feature imaginable is likely to exist.

Mantis shrimp (above) *pierce their prey. The stareye parrot fish* (top right) *nibbles on algae, while the blue-spotted stingray* (right) *eats sea urchins and other bottom-dwelling animals.*

PARTNERS

THE COLORS OF REEF ANIMALS ARE AS diverse and complex as the animals themselves. Divers see—or fail to see—some of the best camouflage on earth. The colors of some reef animals deceive, while other colors advertise.

A fish's color is a key to its identification, but this characteristic can be tricky, since many fish species have the ability to change color almost instantly. Some fish are colored one way when they are young and another way when they become adults. Others change at dusk, replacing their showy daytime look for drab, mottled nighttime colors that conceal the fish as they sleep.

Many reef fish can change color to match their surroundings. Trumpetfish are masters at this. They change color to match their background, and then ambush other fish. Since trumpetfish are long and skinny, parts of their bodies and long snouts may be different colors. A trumpetfish hunting small yellow fish may turn its head yellow while the rest of its body

matches the background. If a prey fish mistakes the trumpetfish's head for one of its own kind, it may soon find itself in the trumpetfish's jaws.

On reefs all over the world, several kinds of small wrasses and gobies are light colored, with a dark blue stripe on each side of their bodies. These fish are full-time cleaners of other, larger fish, and their distinctive coloring seems to advertise their services.

One fish cleaning another, and gaining food in the process, is just one of many partnerships among reef organisms. These relationships are called *mutualistic* because both partners benefit. More than fifty species of reef fish are cleaners. Some only serve as cleaners while young. They have that distinctive stripe on their sides until they are adult, when they get food in other ways. In addition to fish, several kinds of crabs and shrimps, including the red-backed shrimp and the barbershop shrimp, also offer cleaning services.

Reefs have cleaning stations where the cleaner fish (or other cleaners) wait for "customers." Cleaner fish

Motionless, a trumpetfish waits, ready to ambush a small fish that swims near.

perform a sort of dance, displaying their colors over a favorite piece of coral. Sometimes a line of fish waits for service near a cleaning station. The customers often assume odd positions, for example, pointing their bodies head up or head down, and seem to be in a trance. (Diver-photographers have learned that their best chance of getting close to wary fish species comes during cleaning time.)

The fish being cleaned may be large predators, such as jacks or moray eels, that would ordinarily gobble down a goby or other small prey. The partnership is understood, however, and customers even open their mouths so the little cleaners can work within. Cleaners nibble off bits of dead tissue, fungi, and tiny crustaceans that are parasites of fish. They get fed under safe working conditions, and the service they provide is important, too. When biologists removed all cleaner species from isolated reefs, the fish there developed ragged fins as well as body sores and other health problems.

In the Caribbean one species of fish is a fake cleaner. The mimic blenny looks and acts almost exactly like a cleaner wrasse. However, a fish that sees it and pauses to be cleaned is in for a big surprise. The mimic swims up to a soft part of the larger fish and then darts forward, takes a bite, and dashes away. Divers, too, are sometimes nipped by the fangs of these little mimics.

When divers swim close to sea anemones, they may witness another reef partnership. Several species of damselfish, called clownfish, live among the stinging tentacles of anemones. Clownfish always stay near an anemone, eating algae and zooplankton, and flee among its tentacles when a predator approaches. Clownfish are protected from stings by a coating of mucus, while predators that try to catch them are not. Clownfish clearly benefit, but what about their partners? Apparently, anemones gain some protection, as clownfish drive off certain kinds of butterfly fish that feed on anemones. They may also gain nutrients

Cleaner gobies serve a customer, a moray eel.

from food particles and wastes dropped by clownfish.

Some slender little gobies spend almost their entire lives within the tunnels and chambers of large sponges. Other gobies live beneath sea urchins. The gobies clearly gain shelter and food from these relationships, but it is not known if the other organisms do. Another kind of goby has a partnership with the pistol shrimp, in which the fish serves as a lookout out for the shrimp, which has poor eyesight.

Both the fish and the shrimp share a burrow that the shrimp digs. When the shrimp leaves its burrow, it keeps its long antennae in touch with the goby. If danger approaches, the goby dives for the burrow with the pistol shrimp right behind. The two animals are almost always in close contact, a true partnership in survival.

A tomato clownfish is not harmed by an anemone's stinging tentacles.

CHEMICAL WARFARE

CORAL REEFS HAVE FISH AND OTHER creatures that move swiftly, but many reef dwellers move slowly or, like corals themselves, stay put. Somehow they must get food and also defend themselves. Many organisms meet these needs with venoms, which are poisonous chemicals that are injected into victims by means of spines, fangs, or stinging cells.

A study of more than four hundred corals, anemones, and other invertebrates of the Great Barrier Reef found that about three-quarters of these animals were toxic to fish. Coral reefs may be the naturally most poisonous habitats on earth. Of course, many of the toxins—like those in the stinging cells of coral polyps—are meant for small prey. Most pose no threat to humans, though cuts caused by the rough edges of coral colonies heal very slowly. The toxins of other reef animals, however, can be painful or even deadly to people.

Beginning divers are warned not to touch anything and especially to look out for certain toxic animals.

One is the fire coral. It is not named for its color, which is often brownish or yellow, but for the fiery sting of its tentacles. Just brushing against a fire coral can cause intense pain, and a wound that may not heal for months. Fire corals are more closely related to such stinging jellyfish as the dreaded Portuguese man-of-war than to true corals.

Divers are also advised to avoid bristle worms and sea urchins, with their poisonous spines, and sea anemones, with their stinging tentacles. Never pick up a reef animal. Some mollusks, including cone shells and octopuses, kill their prey with toxins. If captured, they defend themselves. Their toxins affect the nervous system and have caused human deaths.

On an Australian beach a teenage boy picked up a blue-ringed octopus to scare his girlfriend. Struggling to get away, the small octopus pecked the youth with its beak. Two hours later the boy was dead.

Careful divers avoid touching most reef life but worry about an accidental encounter with a member

Fire coral is named for the fiery stings given by its tiny tentacles.

of the scorpion fish family. These fish are well camouflaged and highly venomous. (The family includes more than eighty species; the most dangerous ones live on Pacific and Indian Ocean reefs.) Most members of this family are predators that conceal themselves and wait to gobble down smaller fish that swim near. The venoms that coat sharp spines on their fins help these fish defend themselves against rays, sharks, and other predators. In humans these chemicals can cause terrible pain and even death.

Lionfish are members of the scorpion fish family. With their winglike fins spread outward, they look like a sea fan or other soft coral. Sometimes these slow swimmers corner a small fish, using their outspread fins as a barrier to prevent its escape. If a diver swims too close to a lionfish, it doesn't flee. It erects its eighteen venomous spines and stands ready to inflict terrible pain.

Other members of the scorpion fish family are even harder to see. Several kinds of scorpion fish look like clumps of seaweed. They move to the rhythm of currents and waves and are seldom noticed by reef explorers. Another member of this family, the stonefish, looks like a gray stone among other stones, or part of the sandy bottom. It may bury itself almost completely in coral sand and wait

for a small fish or a shrimp to come by.

In his book *Killers of the Seas,* Edward Ricciuti wrote: "I have often watched visitors to the New York Aquarium pause before a tank holding two or three stonefish, and then walk away complaining that there were no fish in the tank."

The spines on a stonefish's back fin act like hypodermic needles, injecting venom from sacks at the bases of the spines. The spines are strong and sharp enough to pierce sneakers, and a person who is stabbed by several spines is usually dead within a few hours. Even a minor wound can be so painful that the victim loses consciousness. In stonefish habitat, which include the shallow waters of reef flats, divers are mighty careful where they step lest they become casualties of the chemical warfare among coral reef animals.

Powerful venom coats the sharp fin spines of the lionfish (left).
Scorpion fish (right) *are well camouflaged and highly venomous.*

More Valuable than We Know

CORAL REEFS HAVE LONG SUPPLIED coastal peoples with seafood, and even building materials. Coral mined from the sea is virtually the only building material available on some Pacific and Indian Ocean islands where little rock occurs. Coral is cut into building blocks, or ground up and added to cement for road construction. The value of reefs goes far beyond these uses, however, as we learn more about reefs and their plant-animal communities.

Most important is the basic structure of reefs and their position offshore of islands and continents. When ocean waves collide with a reef, the waves lose between 70 and 90 percent of their energy. Reefs reduce coastal erosion wherever they occur. They protect not just human communities but also marshes, lagoons, mangrove forests, and other wild habitats. Coral reefs make possible the very existence of such low-lying islands as the Maldives in the Indian Ocean. If sea levels rise as a result of worldwide warming of the atmosphere, coral reefs will be needed more than ever.

Millions of people get food and earn money by catching fish from reef ecosystems. Researchers have learned that coral reefs are nurseries and feeding grounds for fish species that range far from the tropics. As the world population grows and the need for seafood increases, this role of coral reefs will become even more important.

Many people are aware that tropical forests are homes for a rich variety of animal and plant species. Now the value of coral reefs as centers of *biodiversity* is also being recognized. People take delight in this wealth of coral reef life just for its beauty and mystery, but there are other reasons to appreciate it—including even its many stinging animals.

Plant and animal poisons have always been a likely source of medicines and drugs for people. For example, study of venom from scorpions led to the development of a drug for treating strokes, the

By quelling the power of waves, coral reefs protect low-lying islands and coasts from erosion.

sudden attacks that can leave people paralyzed. The toxins of reef animals have great potential for producing new kinds of drugs, including those used to combat inflammations and arthritis. Toxic chemicals from certain sponges and corals slow the growth of cancer cells. In the past few years coral reefs have been recognized as the prime source of natural chemicals that might be useful in treating human diseases. They are also a likely source of a whole new arsenal of chemicals that could be used against insect pests on land.

Coral itself is now used as a substitute for bone in surgery. Pieces of coral are heated until only a porous mineral structure remains. This material can be carved into the shape of the bone to be replaced. It contains a maze of channels that allow real bones to grow into the coral and attach firmly to it. Coral has been used to replace parts of leg and chin bones.

Long-dead stony corals are useful to people in another way—as clues to changes in the earth's climate. Atmospheric scientists are trying to learn about past climate changes so that they can say with greater confidence whether the earth's climate is warming. Drilling into ancient reefs reveals a series of bands, like growth rings in trees, that give clues about the conditions under which corals grew.

The reefs themselves play a role in global climate. Coral polyps remove large amounts of carbon dioxide from ocean waters, which are a storehouse of this gas. According to most atmospheric scientists, increasing amounts of carbon dioxide, methane, and other gases will cause the earth's climate to warm. This global warming could harm reefs and further reduce the amount of carbon dioxide that polyps convert into limestone.

Coral reefs are underwater oases of great beauty, but clearly there is much more to them. They are probably even more valuable than we know already.

Coral reefs are rich with life and still full of mystery.

Saving the Undersea Treasures

In one sense coral reefs are tough. They stand up to the constant slams of ocean waves, and even survive hurricanes. And yet they are fragile habitats. The coral animals themselves are sensitive to changes in sunlight, temperature, and nutrients. Reefs are only as healthy as the water around them, and today that health is declining. Threats to coral reefs have never been greater than they are today.

Since the late 1970s, biologists have noticed reefs in trouble. The problems vary from one place to another. Overfishing has taken a heavy toll in the Philippines, Guam, Indonesia, and the Caribbean. Fish from reefs have been harvested for many thousands of years, but modern methods, such as spear guns, commercial poisons, and even dynamite, make fishing easy, and also highly destructive to reef life. These methods have been outlawed in most places but are still used illegally.

The largest food fish, such as groupers, snappers, and emperors, have been wiped out in many reef areas. Fisherfolk have turned to smaller species and are taking too many of them, also.

As the variety of life on a reef declines, its food webs are affected. Biologists have noticed that overfished reefs in the Caribbean and the Red Sea often have huge populations of sea urchins, which kill corals as they feed on algae. Reefs destroyed by sea urchins become so covered with algae that coral animals often cannot begin new colonies. Biologists suspect that urchin numbers have grown because the fish that prey on them have become scarce.

People like to collect objects from the ocean, and also have a bit of live ocean in their homes. The fastest growing segment of the aquarium industry is the minireef, a saltwater aquarium stocked with reef life.

Almost all reef animals used in home aquariums are captured in the wild, with more than half coming from the Philippines. A lot of them die while being transported or stored in aquarium shops. Many others die after a few weeks or months in aquariums. One reason is the way in which reef fish are sometimes collected. Divers spray sodium cyanide into crevices in order to stun fish hiding within. This poison damages corals; it also harms the liver and other organs of the fish that are collected for sale.

When porcupine fish and other predators of sea urchins are overfished, growing numbers of sea urchins may destroy reefs.

According to several estimates, at least 70 percent of all reef fish caught for aquariums are dead within a year. Some of the species sold cannot even survive away from a real reef. These include cleaner fish, which die of starvation because they need more customers than an aquarium can provide, and butterfly fish, which eat live coral polyps that seldom survive in aquariums, either.

As all of this waste and abuse of reef life has become known, many national and state governments have taken steps to stop it. They regulate fishing, license collectors, outlaw some practices, and set up protected reserves. Some nations forbid the importation of certain reef fish.

Both national and state governments have established coral reef parks and reserves where fishing and collecting is limited or forbidden. They include the Florida Keys National Marine Sanctuary and Ras Muhammad Marine Park, Egypt's first national park. In Belize the Hol Chan Marine Reserve protects a small part of that nation's 140-mile barrier reef, which is the largest reef system in the western hemisphere.

Attempts to protect reefs are often opposed by people whose livelihoods depend on having access to reefs. They include people who harvest food fish, sponges, lobsters, and animals for the aquarium business. In the Florida Keys the protesters include treasure hunters. The area that is now the Florida Keys National Marine Sanctuary is a graveyard for an estimated two thousand sunken ships, including Spanish galleons laden with gold. However, the methods used to locate buried ships can harm reefs. In 1992, when the federal government issued a temporary ban on treasure hunting, about 125 treasure-seeking individuals and small companies protested loudly.

Unfortunately, one of the greatest threats to a healthy, thriving coral reef can be people who come to see it. Exploring reefs with snorkels and especially with scuba (self-contained underwater breathing apparatus) is a popular hobby and a major source of revenue in the tourist and travel businesses. Many divers are not aware of the fragility of live corals or of their slow rate of recovery. When people touch corals or stand on them, the corals die. Marine biologists report seeing patches of dead coral the exact shape of divers' swim fins.

In an instant a dropped boat anchor can break off a quarter century of coral growth. A dragged anchor can plow a swath of death through a reef. Steps are being taken to reduce this damage. At some popular dive places, permanent mooring buoys are being installed so that boats need not use anchors. At the crowded reefs off the Florida Keys, people can be fined for harming reefs while diving or boating. And as the awful damage caused by divers is finally recognized, the tourist and diving industries are doing more to encourage protection of reefs. Each year about a half million people receive scuba training. More and more of them are being taught that diving to coral reefs is not just another sport, like wind surfing or waterskiing, but one that carries a special responsibility.

There is a growing concern about coral reefs among divers and the general public that heartens environmental groups and marine scientists. However, one threat to reefs looms above all of the others. It is the quality of the water in which corals live. Living conditions for corals may be getting worse, not just locally but wherever corals grow.

Water pollution is a special concern in the Florida Keys. Some 700 tons of nutrients enter the water just offshore each year. About half comes from a sewage treatment plant in Key West; the rest leaks from thousands of septic tanks and cesspits. Prevailing currents bring some of these nutrients to Florida's long string of coral reefs that lie 3 1/2 miles from shore at the closest point.

Coral animals thrive in sunlit waters where nutrients are scarce. When waters flowing over reefs carry increased amounts of nutrients, certain kinds of algae benefit and may overwhelm corals. If sea urchins and algae-eating fish are missing, a living reef can disappear fast. Some reefs off the Keys have been lost in this way. There is disagreement among scientists about whether nutrients from human sewage are to blame. They do agree that the reefs are under stress and imperiled.

Beginning in 1987, other signs of reefs in trouble appeared in Florida, throughout much of the Caribbean and elsewhere, including Australia's Great Barrier Reef. Large areas of coral turned white. This is called coral bleaching. It occurs when coral polyps expel the microscopic algae from their cells. This exposes the white limestone skeletons of the polyps.

Corals expel their zooxanthellae when they are under stress. Without the algae they don't get enough food, and cannot grow or reproduce. If conditions do not change, the corals die. If the stressful situation eases, corals regain the algae they need and resume normal life.

Scientists have known about coral bleaching for decades. Usually it is a local change with a specific, identifiable event— hurricane damage, pollution, disease. The coral bleaching of 1987 was large scale. Moreover, it was followed in 1990 by another widespread episode. The cause, at least in the Caribbean and Florida, seemed to have been high water temperatures. Could coral reefs be among the first casualties of *global warming*? Most scientists caution against that conclusion, since coral reefs all over the world are under stress from multiple sources.

Under normal conditions corals have the ability to recover from hurricane damage and other stressful events. However, widespread coral bleaching is not normal, according to studies of ancient coral deposits. If coral bleaching episodes continue to be widespread, coral reefs will die all over the world. This would be a catastrophic loss.

Whatever troubles coral reefs face, it is fair to say that people have caused most of them. We must take steps to save what is left of earth's undersea treasures.

Glossary

algae Simple plants lacking roots, stems, and leaves. Algae include long seaweed and tiny one-celled forms. Unlike fungi, algae are able to make their own food, and are directly or indirectly a vital source of food for all water animals.

biodiversity A term that refers to the variety of living organisms on earth. More than 1.5 million different kinds of *species,* or living things, have been identified so far. The total number of species may reach 30 million.

crustaceans Animals that biologists classify as Crustacea, which have paired, jointed legs and external skeletons. Crustaceans include crabs, lobsters, shrimp, barnacles, and water fleas.

ecosystem All of the living and nonliving parts of a given area in nature; for example, a coral reef, a desert, or even a backyard.

global warming An increase in the atmosphere's temperature caused by human activities such as burning coal, oil, and wood, which add carbon dioxide and other heat-absorbing gases to the atmosphere.

habitat The kind of plant-animal community in which an organism lives. For example, clownfish and parrot fish live in a coral reef habitat.

invertebrates Animals with no *vertebrae,* or backbones. They include insects, spiders, crabs, corals, and *mollusks.*

larva Among fish, the immature form that hatches from an egg and later develops into an adult. Larval fish are also called fry.

mollusks Animals that biologists classify in the large group Mollusca, which includes more than 45,000 species. Clams, snails, slugs, squid, and octopuses are mollusks.

mutualism A relationship between two dissimilar organisms in which both partners benefit. Termites, for example, rely on microscopic protozoans within their bodies to digest the wood they eat. Since the protozoans have a home and a food supply, they benefit, too.

nutrients Substances that are needed for the normal growth and development of an organism. For example, small amounts of certain vitamins and minerals are vital nutrients for good human health.

plankton Tiny drifting plants and animals that live in salt water and fresh water. The phytoplankton, or plants, include *algae* and are the first link of many aquatic food chains. The *zooplankton,* or animals, feed mostly on phytoplankton and are food themselves for fish and other larger animals.

polyp An individual coral animal. Most coral polyps live in colonies, though each animal captures its own food with the tiny tentacles that ring its mouth.

predator An animal that kills other animals for its food.

species A population or many populations of an organism that have characteristics in common, which make them different from individuals of other populations. The members of a species interbreed with one another but not with members of other species. For example, great white sharks mate with other great white sharks but not with hammerhead sharks.

vertebrates Animals with vertebrae, or backbones. They include fish, amphibians, reptiles, birds, and mammals.

zooplankton *See plankton.*

zooxanthellae Algae that usually live within the tissues of coral *polyps.* Both these microscopic plants and the coral animals benefit. Although the relationship is not well understood, it seems that the zooxanthellae provide some of the carbon compounds that make it possible for coral animals to produce limestone.

INDEX